Kate Banks · Pictures by Georg Hallensleben

A GIFT
FROM THE SEA

Frances Foster Books · Farrar, Straus and Giroux · New York

The boy crouched low on the beach.
He picked up a rock hidden in the cool
wet sand and held it in his hand.

He didn't know that the rock had been
spewed from a fiery volcano and cooled
in the shade of a thousand years.

He didn't know that the earth had heaved
and swayed and left the rock
at the foot of a mountain.

He didn't know that when the cold came,
the rock had lain under the weight
of an ice cap in a crisp blue stillness.

"Look," said the boy.
He felt the ridges and grooves of the rock.
He rubbed its rough edges.

He didn't know that when the ice melted,
the rock had become part of a cave.

Or that centuries of rain and wind
had worn away the rock,
changing its shape and form.

He didn't know that in ancient times
a city had risen around the rock.

The boy turned the rock over in his hand.
He studied the lines etched in its curves.

He didn't know that when the ancient city crumbled,
the rock became a landmark for travelers.

He didn't know that in time a wheat field
had grown up around the rock.

The boy took the rock home and placed it
on a shelf beside his box of sea glass.

He didn't know that a river
had swallowed the wheat field
and carried the rock toward the sea.

He didn't know that for a long time
the rock had rested on the ocean floor
near a sunken ship.

Or that, by the light of a full moon,
the rock had been thrust onto the beach.

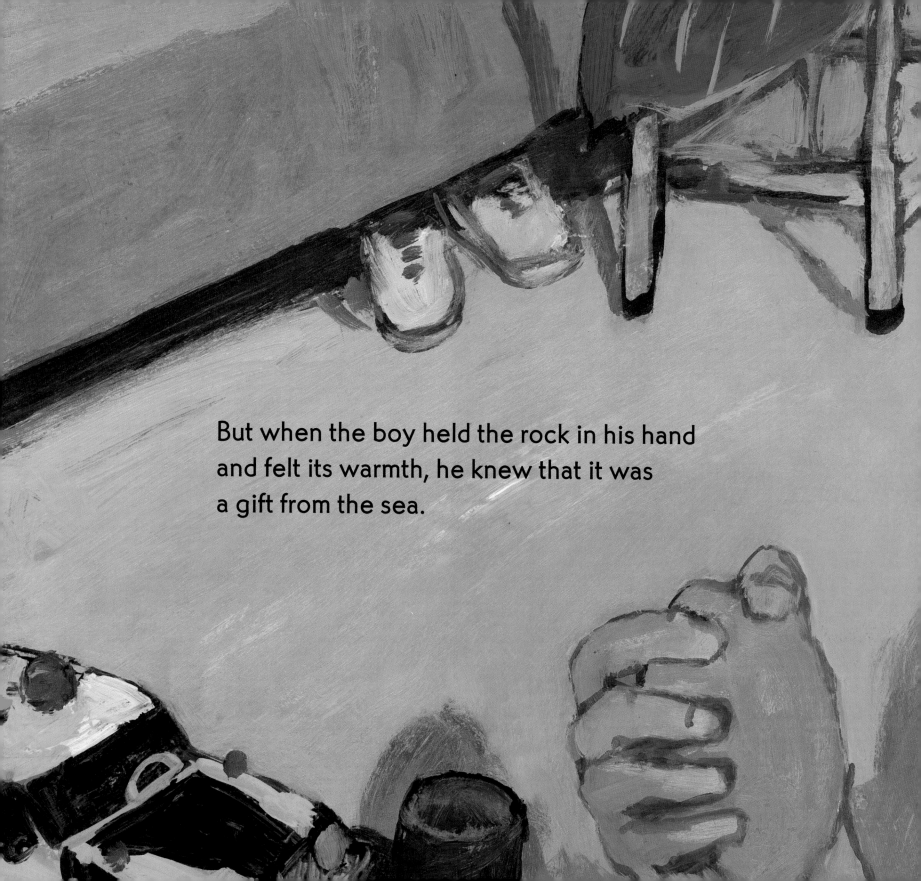

But when the boy held the rock in his hand
and felt its warmth, he knew that it was
a gift from the sea.

Text copyright © 2001 by Kate Banks
Pictures copyright © 1999 by Georg Hallensleben
All rights reserved
Originally published in France under the title
Un don de la mer by Gallimard Jeunesse, 1999
Distributed in Canada by Douglas & McIntyre Ltd.
Printed and bound in Italy
Designed by Judy Lanfredi
First American edition, 2001
1 3 5 7 9 10 8 6 4 2

Library of Congress Cataloging-in-Publication Data

Banks, Kate, 1960—
    [Don de la mer. English.]
    A gift from the sea / Kate Banks ; pictures by Georg Hallensleben.—1st American ed.
        p.   cm.
    Summary: Unaware of its eons-old history, a boy finds a rock and takes it home to a shelf
beside his sea glass and starfish.
    ISBN 0-374-32566-9
    [1. Rocks—Fiction. 2. Seashore—Fiction. 3. Ocean—Fiction.] I. Hallensleben, Georg, ill.
II. Title.

PZ7.B22594 Gi 2001
[E]—dc21

                                                    00-26503